FOR THE YOUNG

AND OLD SOULS

Henri **RENOIR** Rennie

For my beloved Meredith,
without you this would never have
happened, darling!

MEREDIAN

PICTURES & WORDS

Contents

1. FUGGLESTON GREEN

Meredith and I were driving around the United Kingdom, and we passed a little signpost pointing to "Fuggleston Green". We both loved the sound of the name, and just knew there was a story in it. By the time we got to our hotel in the outline had taken shape. By the next morning it was written.

There's something magical about old forests. They're the lungs of the Earth, but in many ways its heart, too. It's important for us all to preserve them.

1. The forest is a place where
things grow.
Big things, like trees.
Little things like mosses and lichens.
In-between things like
bushes and creepers.
Deep inside the heart
of all the plants,
Inside the leaves and branches,
In the buds of moss and
twigs of lichen

Something lives.
If you're very quiet and go to be
amongst the forest
You just might meet it. Or them.
You could hear voices in the ferns.
You could glimpse shapes
amongst the leaves.
Deep in the wood you might find the
Green Man himself.
The forest is a place where
things grow.

*

2. The man had a family, once.
It had been a long time ago.
Sometimes he could remember
his Mum and Dad, and that
made him happy.
Sometimes he couldn't remember
them at all, and that made him sad.
The man had left school too early.
He'd never had a job.
When his parents died he didn't

have a home.
The man spent his days
on the streets, offering a little song
or a shuffling dance.
He spent his nights in the forest.
He slept in a little shelter he made
deep among the trees.
The man talked to the plants – moss,
creepers, bushes, ferns and all.
He talked to all the things that lived
in the forest.
Some of them were things
he realized only he could see.
The man had a family, once.

*

3. The man was troubled.
It had started with an itch, just by
his shoulder.
He would scratch but it wouldn't
go away.
The itch became a lump, and the lump
slowly grew larger and larger.

The man wore a big old loose cloak
to cover the lump.
When he was on the streets, people
thought he was a hunchback.
Eventually the lump looked like a
little head.
It had a face and hair and a beard
That looked like they were made of
twigs and leaves and buds.
On the streets he knew he must
hide it,
But in the forest he would
take off his cloak.
One tired evening he turned to his
new face and said, "Who *are* you?"
The face said, "Fuggleston Green."
The man was troubled.

*

4. The streets were a hard place.
The only plants were sad things
trapped in pots
Or tough little weeds

that fought up through
cracks in concrete and stone.
The man would do a little dance or
sing as people passed.
Kind people would give him
a bit of money.
That meant he could buy something
warm to eat and drink.
If the shopkeeper would serve him,
that is.
Some shopkeepers didn't like beggars.
Some days, if the wind blew up the
streets from the forest
The man could hear Fuggleston Green
softly sing along with him.
They were good days –
the man didn't feel so alone then.
Some days that would be the only
voice he'd hear.
Sometimes people don't talk to the
poor ones, like they aren't
even there.
The streets were a hard place.

*

5. "What a funny man," said the boy
with very short hair.
"Funny peculiar," said the clever girl.
"Funny to look at," said the banker's
son, and the other children laughed.
"It's a bit sad he has to live on the
streets," said the blonde girl.
"He doesn't, you know, he lives in the
forest," said the boy who
wore glasses.
"And it's not sad. It's all his own
fault. My Dad said so,"
Said the banker's son, folding
his arms.
"I like it when he sings with
two voices," said the quiet child,
But nobody ever listened much
to the quiet child.
"My Dad said he should be Off The
Streets," said the banker's son,
And threw a pebble at the man.
The man didn't move

when the pebble hit him,
or the next one, or the next.
"It's like throwing stones at a stick –
we should call him the stick man!"
"What a funny man," said the boy
with very short hair.

*

6. They ran and ran and ran..
The man had had enough of the
children's laughs, and their pebbles,
So he'd hurried back to the forest
where he felt safe.
As they watched him scurry away
the children had talked
amongst themselves.
"Let's follow the stick man!"
said the banker's son.
"Maybe he lives in a stick house,"
laughed the boy with very short hair.
"Maybe he's really rich and has a
proper house hidden there,"
said the clever girl.

So they'd run into the forest
after the man.
They ran deeper into the woods than
any of them had ever been.
The clever girl pointed out some
plants with very long names.
They pushed through bushes and
clambered over creepers.
They got near the little shelter
where the man lived, and
could see him there.
He didn't see them as he
took off his cloak and talked
to Fuggleston Green.
They ran and ran and ran.

*

7. Looking at something isn't the
same as seeing it.
The children were huddled together
at the end of the street.
"He's an ugly man
with a lump on his shoulder,"

said the banker's son.
"I'm sure it had a face," said the boy
who wore glasses.
"I'm sure it talked,"
said the blonde girl.
"Well, I'm not scared,"
said the banker's son.
"We should go back and have
a proper look.
We were just taken by surprise.
There's nothing dangerous
in the forest.
There's no such thing as monsters,"
said the banker's son.
So the next day he led them all
back into the forest.
The sun shining through the leaves
made little patches of light
around them.
The clever girl pointed out more
plants that she knew long names for.
Looking at something isn't the
same as seeing it.

*

8. "Can you tell us more about the
forest?" asked the blonde girl.
"Later," said the clever girl.
"We're nearly at his shelter."
They saw the man talking to
Fuggleston Green, and some
flickering green shapes.
"He's got a hump on his shoulder
and he talks to himself,"
said the banker's son.
"It's a little green man,"
said the blonde girl.
"It's the forest that's talking,"
said the quiet child,
But nobody ever listened much
to the quiet child.
They crept closer to the man and the
flickering little green shapes.
"Um… hello," said the boy
who wore glasses.
"Hello," said the man.
"Hello," said Fuggleston Green.

"This is a *Quercus robur* you know,"
said the clever girl.
"I know it's an oak tree that's
hundreds of years old,
And it's where I live," said the man
and Fuggleston Green, together.
"Can you tell us more about
the forest?" asked the blonde girl.

*

9. They talked about the forest
and they listened.
Well, some of the children did.
"You're imagining things!"
said the banker's son.
"I don't think this can be quite real,"
said the clever girl.
"We must be near some mushrooms
that can make you
have strange dreams."
Fuggleston Green said,
"You are clever, but not yet wise."
"If someone chops you or cuts you,

does it hurt?" asked the blonde girl.
"Yes," said one of the little green
shapes. "But we heal and
grow back slowly."
"This is silly – we should go home,"
said the banker's son.
"Why do the leaves fall down?"
asked the boy who wore glasses.
"The leaves become the soil and
feed the trees they fell from,"
said a shape.
"He's just an ugly man with an ugly
lump!" said the banker's son,
and ran away.
"I'm sorry I carved my name
in one of you,"
said the boy with very short hair.
They talked about the forest
and they listened.

*

10. "He touched me,"
said the banker's son.

"The man touched me
and I didn't like it."
The banker's son knew it wasn't true,
But he wanted to get the man
into trouble.
He was angry at the man.
The other boys and girls had
stopped listening to him.
They were listening to
the man instead,
Or to Fuggleston Green, at least.
Fuggleston Green, who the banker's
son couldn't even see.
That made him angry, too -
Angry at the children who could see
Fuggleston Green and his friends,
And especially angry at the man.
So he got the man into trouble
with a lie.
"He touched me,"
said the banker's son.

*

11. The policeman was angry.
He'd read about people who did
bad things to children.
He didn't like that at all.
The banker's son had complained,
And the banker was an
important person.
The police were expected to Do
Something about the man.
The policeman didn't like beggars.
He didn't like the forest, either.
He marched up to the man, who was
doing a little dance in the street.
"What have you been doing
to the children?"
demanded the policeman.
The man looked surprised.
"They visit me in the forest," he said.
"They talk to me
and I show them things."
The policeman was angry.

*

12. "I must run," thought the man.
The policeman had tried to
grab his shoulder
But Fuggleston Green had moved
And the big cloak slipped from
under the policeman's hand.
"What an ugly lump he has!" thought
the angry policeman.
The man was afraid, so he ran for
the safety of the forest.
"Only guilty people run away,"
thought the policeman.
He didn't stop to think that
frightened people run away, too.
The policeman started to
chase the man
But his feet got tangled in the cloak
that had fallen off.
So the man got a good head start.
The streets were hard as
his feet pounded on them.
He wanted the softness of
the moss and leaves.
"I must run," thought the man.

13. The forest is deep and green.
The policeman lost sight of the man
as they ran.
A creeping vine caught
the man's ankles.
He fell on the moss and lay still.
Leaves fell, covering him
and Fuggleston Green.
The policeman didn't see them
as he ran past.
He didn't see them when he turned
around and angrily went
back to the streets.
Nobody ever saw the man again.
Nobody except for the flickering
green things.
The man and Fuggleston Green
lay softly on the ground
under the leaves.
They sang together softly as they
fed the forest.
The green things danced as

the forest grew.
The man couldn't remember feeling
so happy or so loved.
The forest is deep and green.

*

14. The quiet child was troubled.
The children had gone back
to the forest,
All except the banker's son.
They'd looked high and low
for the man
and Fuggleston Green.
"I'm afraid he's really gone," the
clever girl had said.
"The police have scared him away,"
the boy with very short hair had said.
"He's deep inside the forest,"
the quiet child had said
But nobody ever listened much
to the quiet child.
The quiet child kept going back
to the forest, all alone.

The quiet child could see the little
flickering green shapes
And the flickering shapes listened
to the quiet child.
One night in bed, the quiet child
noticed a tiny little itch.
The forest is a place where things
grow.
The quiet child wasn't troubled at all.

.o0o.

2. THE BULLDOZER PEOPLE

I was brought up to wait patiently in a queue. To be polite, stand aside or stand up for people who needed that courtesy. I don't always get it right, but I try. I suppose that makes me very old-fashioned.

Meredith and I were travelling in Europe, and discovered that there are a lot of people who don't think, or behave, the same way that I was brought up to. (Actually, those people are all over the world...)

Instead of having me get angry and behaving as badly as they did (which was very tempting!) Meredith encouraged me to write about it instead. This is what came out.

In a distant and interesting corner of the world there's a high plateau.

Scattered along the top of the plateau are a number of little towns. They're

very old, and the people who live in
them have been there for a long, long
time.

  Not many people climb up the plateau, and those who do usually wind
up deciding that they really like one
or other of the little towns they find
up there. So they stay, and the plateau
towns remain largely unknown to the
outside world.

  But this is one of their stories.

  At one end of the plateau was a town
named Block. The people who lived
in Block were big, heavy people with
loud voices. They had big square
heads and big square bodies and they
shouted a lot. They were like walking
bulldozers.

  The bulldozer people of Block always seemed to be busy. They were

impatient, and would push each other
around and shove each other out of
the way in their hurry to get to places
and do things.

They would shout over the top of
each other because each one of them
knew that whatever they had to say
was absolutely the most important
thing that could be said right at that
moment.

All of the pushing and shoving and
crowding meant that Block itself got
very dirty and rundown. Walls started
to crack, the footpaths started to sag,
things broke down and didn't get repaired because everyone was too busy
demanding that someone else should
do something about it.

Eventually there came a time when
Block started to become too worn out,

crowded and noisy even for the people who'd lived there a long time.

"Block isn't good enough for us now! We should visit somewhere else and see what's there!" cried some of the big square people.

A few of them travelled along the plateau to the next town – a quiet place named Sekund. There was more space there, and the people weren't very good at standing up to the big square bodies of the bulldozer people when they started behave the way they did at home.

The news got back to Block quickly, and more and more of the big square people moved along the plateau away from their old homes and into Sekund.

They pushed their way in. They pushed the Sekunders out of their way, or pushed them around and shouted at them.

"We are visitors you know! You're supposed to treat us well – bring us food and something to drink!" they would shout.

Some of the Sekunders thought that this was a way to behave that really got results, so they started to do the same things. They pushed people around and shouted and demanded that things be done for them.

They never even noticed that the more they behaved like this, the more their bodies and heads started to change shape. They were starting to look just like the people from Block as well as act like them.

The poor little town of Sekund hadn't been built for rough treatment. The streets were narrower than those in Block. Shouting voices echoed and sounded even louder, and the walls and footpaths quickly started to crack and crumble.

 Soon many of the big square bodied people had started to move along the plateau again, pushing their way into another town, and another after that.

 Everywhere they went, they pushed and shoved and bullied.

"We are visitors! We demand to be served properly!" they would shout at the local people.

 Some people did their best to keep out of the way, some started to behave the same way, and others just got trampled on.

 All too soon, the big loud bulldozer

people from Block, and others who behaved just like them, had moved all the way along the plateau.

  Some of the folks in those towns tried to stand up to the Block people. They got run over, shouted at and pushed aside.

  The big loud square bodied people really were just like bulldozers, shoving and squashing anyone and anything in their way.

  The Mayor of the town of Quailville tried to talk to the people from Block when they first arrived.

"You can have some of our town all to yourselves, and we will live peacefully in the other part," he offered.

  The Block people agreed that was a good idea. But it didn't take long

before their part of Quailville got
noisy and crowded and unpleasant.

"The other part of Quailville looks
much nicer," they said.

So they pushed their way into the rest
of the town. The poor Mayor was just
another person to be pushed aside.
`

"This is no way to treat visitors! Why
didn't you let us have this bit of the
town? It's much nicer!" shouted one
of the bulldozer people.

"It used to be," said the Mayor in a
sad, quiet voice as he looked around
at the noisy, shoving crowd. But the
people from Block didn't hear him.

So they kept moving along the plateau, finding nice unspoiled places
and spoiling them. Not deliberately,
of course, but it never occurred to

the Block people that their noise, and their pushing, and their rudeness, was really the cause of the problems they kept trying to leave behind.

Eventually they got to the very last town on the plateau. It was a very old town called Terminus.

The very polite people of Terminus welcomed them.

"You're welcome to come in, but please be gentle. All of our town is very old and fragile," they said.

"Yes, yes, sure. Now get out of the way!" replied the people from Block.

With a sigh the polite people of Terminus stood back and let the bulldozer people pass before they could be pushed aside or crushed.

Block people all across the plateau soon heard how easy it was to get into Terminus. They rushed there, pushing themselves along, pushing each other out of the way, and shouting as if being louder would help get them there sooner.

They pushed down the gates and pushed over the old fragile walls to get in.

Again the polite people tried to give a warning. "Please be careful – all of Terminus is old and fragile," they said.

Most of the bulldozer people didn't even bother to say, "Yes, sure."

They either ignored the polite people, or pushed them out of the way, or shouted at them to get something because they were visitors and expected to be treated well.

Without the people from Block even noticing, the polite people quietly got right out of their way – right out of Terminus, in fact.

The people who used to be the Terminites stood some way away from where their gates had been, shaking their heads sadly. Inside the town, the Block people were rumbling around, pushing and shoving each other and shouting for somebody to come and serve them.

Then suddenly above the terrible noise of the pushing and shoving and shouting came an even louder, more terrible noise. The people of Terminus had warned that all of their town was old and fragile. That included even the ground on which it had been built. The end of the plateau collapsed

under the strain. Terminus and the big
square bulldozer people of Block fell
hundreds of feet to their ruin.

  The polite people made their way
back along the plateau to all the places where those from Block had been.
Places like Quailtown and Sekund –
even the remains of Block itself.

  Gradually the damage in all those
towns was repaired. The people
who were left treated each other with
respect – they'd all learned a lesson
from Block.

  The plateau was shared by everyone,
and became just the best and friendli-
est place in the world to live.

  But they kept that quiet. They knew
that there were other bulldozer people
in the world.

.o0o.

33

3. FLIGHT

My Dad introduced me to puns from a very early age, for which I'm very grateful. (I'm not sure that everyone else I know agrees.)

Since I was little, I've known that every cemetery I see is "the dead centre of town, and people are dying to get in there". Sorry.

It's a wonderful, if sometimes confusing thing about the English language, that one word can have multiple meanings.

A dozen stone steps that cling to the side of a shattered old castle -

A flight of stairs.

An owl that swoops, wings extended and talons outstretched –

A flight of a bird.

A mouse that scurries, head down, as

fast as it can to hide under the stone –

A flight from danger.

A mouse that climbs up onto the
stairs, waves a defiant little fist and
shouts its anger at the owl –

A flight of fancy.

.o0o.

4. LUCIUS LONGPOCKETS

Have you ever noticed that "Grimm's Fairy Tales" are often very GRIM tales?

I suppose that's the point of 'morality tales'. Actions and behaviours have consequences, and to make a point they're often serious consequences. This is one of my morality tales. I know people like Lucius, and I'm sure you do too.

It was written in a Northern Hemisphere winter, which is why I was thinking about snow. It's a little bit chilling...

Lucius Lawrence was his name, but people called him Lucius Longpock- ets because he seemed to have so much trouble reaching for his wallet.

The same people called his poor little wife Nodding Nora, because whatever Lucius said, however outrageous or silly or rude, she would just nod.

Smile her sweet little smile and nod.

Lucius did not believe in paying for anything he could get for free.

"Why should I buy a bottle of water from you?" he snapped at the man in the store. "You have a tap – I'll get my water from that! Cos *that*'s free!"

"Why should I pay to buy a car, or the terrible expense of running one? Why should I pay to ride a bus or a train, full of people I wouldn't like anyway?" he said. "I'll ride my pushbike – cos *that*'s free!"

Lucius still had the bicycle his parents had given him many years earlier. He did his own maintenance work on it. He patched the tyres for as long as he could before he'd finally have to buy a new tyre because there wasn't enough left of the old tyre to patch.

He greased the chain and all the joints with the grease from Nora's kitchen – the grease that was so thick and black and horrible that even he wouldn't eat food cooked in it. Nora would nod and smile sweetly at him, knowing that this week she would get to buy some new cooking oil.

Lucius only had three sets of clothes. He had his 'everyday' clothes, which he would wear every day from Monday to Saturday. He had his stripey pyjamas, that he would wear to bed every night. And he had his Sunday clothes, which he would wear once per week while Nora washed the other clothes.

She would wash his stripey pyjamas first, so that they would be dry in time for Lucius to wear them on Sunday night. Then she would wash his 'everyday' clothes so that they could dry during the day and overnight, ready for him to wear them first thing on Monday.

Nora had a few more changes of clothes than Lucius, but she made sure that they looked like each other so he wouldn't notice and complain about her spending money.

They still lived in the little house that Lucius' parents had owned. There wasn't a lot of room, but there was only the two of them. The house was old, though, and some of it was rather worn-out.

Lucius didn't like having to pay tradesmen to fix things. He was quite clever, and still quite fit so he did most things around the house himself. He fixed the plumbing when it was needed, and planed the doors when the damp weather warped them and they wouldn't quite shut properly. He wouldn't buy new windows – he would put putty around the panes if they started to rattle in the wind, and put tape over any cracks in the glass.

He would ride his bicycle to the local rubbish tip, and fill up his carry basket with things other people had thrown away that he could use to fix the house. Once he did four trips in a day to bring back a small stack of roof tiles. They were old and a bit damaged and might not quite fit his roof, but they were in slightly better condition than some of the very old ones that were already on the little house.

"And best of all, they're *free*," he explained to Nora as he set up his ladder to repair the roof.

Nora smiled sweetly at him and nodded.

One very cold winter their fridge
broke down. Nora worried that their
food would spoil. She called a serviceman and explained what had
happened. When she had told him all
the details, including how very old the
fridge was, the man made sad little
"Tsk tsk tsk" noises down the phone.

"I don't think it can be repaired,"
he said sadly. "It's very hard to find
parts for a machine that old, and
they're usually expensive. I'm afraid
it would be cheaper for you to buy a
new fridge."

Later, after dinner, Nora told Lucius
what the serviceman had said. He
wasn't pleased, but he had an idea.

"Why should I pay to get another one
now? That can wait until summer
when the sales are on. There's lots of
snow on the ground outside – we can

store our food in that to keep it cold, cos *that*'s free."

 Nora paused for a moment. She didn't nod, and her smile slipped a bit.

 "Are you sure that's a good idea, Lucius? It might be a little – inconvenient," she said.

 Lucius waved his hand, dismissing her concern.

 "There's a nice deep drift of snow under the old tree. That should make it easy for you to find stuff when you need it. I'll put everything in those plastic bags we get for free from the supermarket and move it all now. You take yourself off to bed," he said, feeling quite generous in offering to do the job himself.

 Nora wasn't too keen on having to

dig food and drink out of the snow
whenever she wanted something,
but she nodded and said, "Very well,
dear."

As she went to go to her room Lucius
called out from the doorway, "Don't
lie there reading too late, please. You
know the electricity bill is expensive
enough this time of year."

Nora nodded. She only read two
pages of her favourite book before she
turned out the light. She didn't mind
– she knew the story well, having read
it several times. One day she hoped
they might buy some more books,
even if it was from a second-hand
shop.

She rolled over and went to sleep
listening to the sound of Lucius' foot-
steps as he went back and forth into
the snow-covered garden.

"Whew! Only two more bags to go!" Lucius said to himself as he pushed snow over a bag of sausages.

He went to lean against the old tree and catch his breath, but he slipped slightly on the snow and his hand hit the trunk of the tree quite hard.

The old tree shook with the impact, and snow fell from the old branches. Some of it fell on Lucius, and a lot fell on the roof of the house.

Several of the tiles that didn't fit very well came loose, and as they slid free a great big pile of snow also slipped – right off the roof and onto Lucius Longpockets.

"Gosh! That's freez…" was all he managed to say.

One of the roof tiles bopped him on

the head and knocked him out, but
there was so much snow all over and
around him he didn't fall over. He
just stood there, beside the stash of
grocery bags, wet and coated in snow.

 More flakes started to fall gently
from the sky overnight, covering
Lucius like a snowman. He froze to
death without even knowing it.

 Nora was very sad to lose him of
course. She would think of Lucius
and sigh over a chocolate biscuit and
a cup of tea made
with milk from her nice new fridge, as
she read one of her new books.

But she'd smile her sweet little smile
and nod sadly when friends would
say, "At least now, *you*'re free."

.o0o.

5. FIFTY WAYS TO SAY "THANK YOU"

Wherever in the world I'm visiting, I try to learn a tiny bit of the local language - enough to hopefully keep me out of trouble.

Being polite is usually appreciated any-where, so while "Hello" is important, I think that finding out the local words for "Please" and "Thank you" can matter even more. And I did include my own favourite.

Masvita   baraka laufik
kyai zoo tin baa dai   aw kohn

doh je   meitaki   hvala   dekuji

amasay ganala   motashakkeram
vinaka

kiitos   merci   tapadh leat   danke
ehvkhahreesto   aabhar

mahalo   shalom   kurssurnurm

dalu   terimah kasi
domo arigato gozaimasu

goh mab seumnida   paldies   achiu
xiexie

bayarlalaa   shukran   takk
dziekuje   obrigado

multumesc   spasiba   hvala
ndatenda   istuti

kea leboha   gracias   asante
nandri   khop khoon

thoo jaychay   barkallaoo feek
tesekkur ederim

caym on   enkosi   aagbabire
ngiyabonga

a huge great HUG!

.o0o.

6. THE MAGIC SATCHEL

Another 'morality tale'. It's set mostly in Marrakesh, in Morrocco, which is itself a pretty magical place.

That's part of what inspired this story. That, and watching some people who really didn't seem to understand what "enough" means.

Gavin and Glenys lived in a nice little house in a nice little small town.

It really was quite a small house, and it was a bit old, but it was well looked after and had everything they needed. It felt very safe and comfortable. They both really rather loved their little old house, though neither of them really said so much.

They both had good jobs in the nearby city, and they both worked hard.

One evening after a long day at work
they looked at each other and said,
"We need a holiday!"

So they booked a flight to Marrakesh,
because it sounded far away and exciting and a bit magical.

And so it was – very exciting and just
a bit magical.

They visited beautiful gardens right
on the edge of the desert. They saw
grand old buildings with walls and
floors decorated with gorgeous tiles in
every colour you can imagine. And
they went to the great big marketplace
called the *souk*.

Gavin and Glenys were very excited
by the *souk*. There was so much to
see, and to buy! There were clothes,
and shoes, and jewellery, and lamps,
and carpets and furniture and mirrors

and… and… well, lots of things!

The men who owned the market stalls would ask a high price for their goods, and Glenys would laugh and say, "Oh, you funny man!" before offering a much lower price.

And the men who ran the stalls would laugh and suggest a better price, and they would suggest prices to each other until either they agreed or Gavin and Glenys would shrug, smile and walk away.

That's called "haggling" and it's how the *souk* works in Marrakesh.

Glenys was very good at haggling, and soon Gavin found himself struggling to carry several bags of things they'd bought.

"Let's sit down for a bit, please!"

he said, mopping the sweat from his
forehead.

So they sat at a shady little stall and
had some pastries and mint tea in
glass cups.

Gavin looked down at all the bags of
shopping at his feet. "Do we really
need all these things?" he wondered
out loud.

"I suppose not," admitted Glenys,
"but they're all so pretty. They'll
make our little old house look really
lovely."

"That's true," agreed Gavin.

They both loved their little house, but
did like the idea of making it look a
bit grander.

"I just wish it was easier to carry

around all the things we want," said Gavin, taking the final sip of his mint tea.

Glenys had a puzzled look on her face.

"I didn't notice that stall before," she said, pointing to a tiny little market stall a little way from where they were sitting.

Gavin looked over. "It's just another bag stall," he said with a shrug.

"I don't know. That one looks a bit – different. A bit special I think," Glenys replied. "Let's go take a look."

Standing in front of the stall was Ali Ghalee Bezzaf, whose hair was long and whose beard was silver. He wore long silver earrings and a long black robe with gold patterns sewn on its edges.

Ali Ghalee Bezzaf was really a *jinni* – a magic spirit – but he wasn't about to tell Gavin and Glenys that.

"Welcome to my humble stall," he said as they entered.

Gavin held onto all the shopping bags while Glenys had a little look around. It was a small stall, and there wasn't very much to look at.

"You have many bags, sir," said Ali Ghalee Bezzaf to Gavin.

"You're right there," agreed Gavin. "I don't suppose you have a magic bag that'd make it easier to carry them?" he said, with a smile.

Ali Ghalee Bezzaf gave a small bow and smiled.

"I have just as you wish, sir," he said,
and reached under the little table he
used as a counter.

He pulled out a beautiful leather satchel. It had intricate patterns
worked into the leather of the flap that
closed the bag. One pattern had been
embellished with red paint, another
with blue.

Glenys looked at the bag and couldn't
help but go, "Ooh! Look at the workmanship! This bag is lovely!"

"Thank you, madam," said Ali Ghalee Bezzaf. "But it is more than
that. This is a very special piece of
workmanship – as you requested, it is
magic."

Glenys and Gavin both looked at him
very doubtfully.

"I will show you!" he said, smiling
and stroking his beard. On his little
table was a large round stone that he
used as a paperweight.

 He handed the satchel to Gavin so
he could feel the weight of it – the
bag was remarkably light for its size.
Then he placed the big stone inside
the satchel, where it hung heavily
from Gavin's arm.

 Still smiling, Ali traced the red pattern on the satchel's flap with a finger,
and said, "*Shukran! Shukran!*"

 Gavin looked astonished – suddenly
the bag was as light as before. He
looked inside. "Hey! The stone's
vanished!" he said.

"Well, that is a clever trick," admitted
Glenys, "but it doesn't really help us
very much. What's the good of

having our shopping disappear?"

Ali Ghalee Bezzaf smiled again and said, "It will not disappear, madam. It will just be in a safe place."

He traced the blue pattern on the satchel's flap, and said, "*Shukran! Shukran!*"

Gavin staggered slightly as the weight of the stone suddenly returned to the bag.

"Just think of the thing that you want returned, and there it will be," Ali explained.

Gavin and Glenys looked at each other, their eyes wide.

"Does it have… a limit?" Gavin asked.

Ali shrugged, and took the long pole he used to get bags down from the very top shelf of his stall. He put one end of the pole into the satchel, traced the red design and said, "*Shukran! Shukran!*"

The pole slipped into the bag like it was slipping into a well. The flap of the satchel fell shut.

"May I?" asked Gavin.

Ali nodded.

Gavin pictured in his mind the long pole, traced the blue pattern with a finger and said, "*Shukran! Shukran!*"

He reached into the satchel, and with a look of delighted surprise drew out the pole. He handed the pole back to Ali with a little bow. "It's wonderful!" he said.

Glenys took the satchel from Gavin and turned it around in her hands. She examined the stitching and examined the leather, top and bottom, back, front and sides.

"Will it wear out?" she finally asked.

Ali Ghalee Bezzaf shook his head, his long silver earrings jangling. "No, it will never wear out," the *jinni* replied, "but you must use it wisely. It is not good to be greedy with it. You should never want more than enough."

"Of course, of course," said Glenys and Gavin together, both nodding quickly while they imagined all the things they could put in the satchel.

"How much is it?" asked Glenys, expecting a very high price and preparing to haggle.

"How much will you pay?" replied Ali.

 Glenys blinked in surprise. She looked at Gavin, who shrugged.

"Um… twenty *dirham*?" she suggested cautiously.

"Is that what you think it is worth?" asked Ali Ghalee Bezzaf.

 'It's worth a lot more than that!' is what Glenys thought to herself. But what she said was, "Well, perhaps a little more than that."

 She was surprised to hear herself admit even that – this was not haggling like she'd experienced before!

 Ali smiled and said, "Twenty *dirham* is enough. It is not good to be greedy."

Glenys handed Ali the money, while Gavin began putting the things they'd already bought into the satchel, tracing the red design, and saying, "*Shukran! Shukran!*" over and over again.

As Glenys took a turn at putting things into the bag, Gavin turned to Ali and asked, "By the way - what does that word *shukran* mean?"

"It is the greatest magic word in the world," said Ali Ghalee Bezzaf. "It is how we say 'thank you' in Morocco."

Gavin smiled and said, "Well, *shukran* to you, then!"

The two exchanged bows. "Enjoy your time in Marrakesh, sir and madam. Travel wisely," said the *jinni*.

"Oh, we will!" they both exclaimed,

and laughed as they walked off to explore more of the *souk*.

The next day they explored more, and bought more. Glenys was very good at haggling, and Gavin was starting to get the hang of it too, so they got a lot of things at very good prices.

"You know," said Gavin, "we could charge a lot more than we paid for these things if we sold them at home."

"That's a good idea!" said Glenys, so they started buying even more.

 They looked at a very big, fancy carpet. "It'll never fit in our front room," said Glenys.

"But it will fit very well in old Colonel Houndstooth's big house. I'm sure he'll buy it from us at a good price," said Gavin.

So they bought the big fancy carpet, and had it rolled up tight so that one end would fit into the magic satchel.

When they left the carpet stall they ducked into a little alleyway of the souk so no one would see them. Gavin traced the red design, and quietly said, *"Shukran! Shukran!"* Just like slipping into a well, the carpet slid into the bag and disappeared.

Gavin and Glenys thought the carpet seller hadn't seen them, but he'd noticed them through a tiny window in his stall. If they were worried about their magic satchel being stolen though, they needn't have been.

The carpet seller shook his head worriedly when he saw the magic at work. "Ali Ghalee Bezzaf!" he said to himself. "I have enough!"

That night in their hotel, Gavin and Glenys looked at their suitcases.

"We certainly won't have to pay an Excess Baggage charge when we fly home!" laughed Gavin.

They got a few things back out of the satchel to admire them in the peace and quiet of the hotel room, then put them back in whatever safe place they went to.

"You know, if we had a bag like that each, we could get a lot more stuff. For the house, I mean," said Glenys. "There were those lovely big brass lamps I wanted. And those blue and white ceramic pots, and one or two of those mirrors in the elegant silver frames."

"We could fit all those in this bag, I think," said Gavin.

"But if we had one each we could both shop for the things we want. We've only got another two days here to get the things we want!"

So the next day they searched the *souk* for the bag stall of Ali Ghalee Bezzaf, but they couldn't find it. Neither had thought to ask Ali his name, so they couldn't tell anyone who they were looking for.

Of course, Glenys and Gavin didn't know that Ali Ghalee Bezzaf was a *jinni*, and if any of the other stallholders they spoke to knew, they weren't telling.

They went to where they'd had the mint tea and pastries, and looked along the way to where they thought was the right place. There was a stall selling shoes and slippers with curly toes, and next door was a stall selling copper pots and pans.

 When they tried to ask those two
stall holders about the little bag stall
the two sellers shook their heads and
waved their hands.

 Glenys was quite cross – so cross
she didn't even buy any of the copper
pans that she'd really quite admired.

"We've wasted more than half the day
looking for that silly stall. It can't
have just vanished!" she snapped.

 Gavin looked at the magic satchel,
into which things disappeared. "I'm
not so sure about that," he said quietly. "Still, we've got this one and it's
worked well for us so far."

"That's true," Glenys admitted. "But
I wanted more."

"We'll get more," said Gavin. "We've got the rest of today and tomorrow to find the things we want."

So they walked up and down and around and around the *souk*. They haggled as hard as they could, and kept ducking around corners and into quiet nooks to cram big items into the satchel without being seen.

The one or two locals who might have noticed them using the satchel muttered, "Ali Ghalee Bezzaf!" under their breath and quickly looked away.

By the end of their last day in Marrakesh, Glenys had lots of brass lamps and ceramic pots and mirrors, and much more besides. Gavin had bought decorative wood carvings and ornaments. He'd also bought a lot of rugs, thinking it would be nice to have a carpet selling business as well as his normal good job.

Gavin and Glenys had said, "*Shukran! Shukran!*" so often, they just about forgot what it meant. They'd stopped thinking about the magic and appreciating it – they were just using it.

Finally they got on the plane and left Marrakesh. As they sat in the taxi on their way home from the airport they patted the magic satchel and congratulated themselves on how clever they'd been, fitting so much in.

But when the taxi turned into their little street in their little town, the police had blocked it off halfway along, with yellow and black 'Do Not Cross' tape.

"What can have happened?" cried Glenys in concern.

With the taxi stopped at the tape,
Gavin quickly paid the driver. They
grabbed their luggage, which of
course was very light because they'd
put all their clothes and belongings in
the magic satchel, and dashed down
the street.

They stopped and looked in horror at
the remains of their home.

All the things they had bought and
crammed into the satchel had gone
to the safest place they knew – their
own nice little house in their nice little
town.

All the things – the carpets, the mirrors, the pots, the clothes - wood,
glass, metal, heavy cloth, thick earth-
enware – had been landing on the
floor of their front room. The weight
had been too much for the old timber
and it had collapsed.

Without the floor to support it, the
wall of the front room had collapsed
– door, windows and all. And without
the front wall to hold it up, of course
the ceiling and the roof came down.

The little cottage they had loved was
a wreck, crushed by the weight of all
the things they'd bought.

All the things that Gavin and Glenys
just *wanted* had ruined the things that
they loved and needed – the things
that had been enough.

.o0o.

7. EGGS

A mate of mine is a farmer. A while ago he was lamenting to me about how many of the 'city kids' who came to visit his place on school trips really have no idea of where food actually comes from.

I figured there were stories in that. Here's the first.

"Do you know where eggs come from?" the cook asked Nicky.

"Mum keeps them in the door of the fridge."

"Okay, before they go into the fridge – where do they come from?"

 Nicky thought for a moment. "Umm… the supermarket."

"Do you know where the shop gets eggs from?"

"From a farm," said Nicky, remembering something in a book.

"Yes, often they do. How do the farmers get the eggs?"

"Does they grow them? Is that what an eggplant is?"

 The cook laughed. "No, that's a type of vegetable. Eggs come from chickens."

"Oh! Um… how do the chickens get them?"

"They lay them. Female chickens start to lay eggs when they're about twenty weeks old…" the cook started to explain.

 Nicky interrupted. "Wait… what do you mean, 'lay' them? Where does the egg come from?"

"Well, er, out of the chicken's bottom."

"What? Like poop? Ee-uuw!"

"Eggs and poop do come out of the
same hole, but that's okay – they
come from different places inside the
chicken and don't get mixed up together."

"Okay… if you're sure about that,"
said Nicky, looking uncertainly at an
egg on the kitchen bench.

"Definitely!"

"So why do the chickens lay these
eggs?"

"Something inside the chicken's body
makes it produce eggs regularly…"

"How regularly?"

"It varies between chickens. Some might be once or twice per week. When a chicken is young and healthy it might be about every 25 hours."

"There are 24 hours in a day, right? So the chicken lays an egg every day almost!" Nicky was good with numbers.

"Yes. If she lays her very first egg at ten o'clock on a Monday morning, the next will pop out at eleven on Tuesday, then noon on Wednesday, and so on. But most chickens only lay eggs during the daytime, so when that pattern gets to when it's dark she'll stop, and lay her next egg in the morning when it's light."

"Okay, that's when – but *why* is she making them?"

"If there's a rooster spending time

with the chicken, then some of those eggs might get what's called 'fertilized'. That means that a chick grows inside the egg. That's how we get new chickens. But most eggs don't get fertilized, so there are lots more eggs than chickens."

"Otherwise we'd have dozens and dozens of chickens in the supermarket instead of all those eggs. Do white eggs come from white chickens, and brown eggs from brown chickens?"

"Not necessarily. Black chickens don't lay black eggs! Different breeds usually lay slightly different coloured eggs, and each individual chicken will produce pretty much the same colour. Sometimes a bit darker or lighter, or with little speckles – depending on what they've been eating."

"So… if chickens make eggs to make

more chickens… where did the first chicken come from?”

“Or, where did the first egg come from? I don’t think anyone has ever quite figured that one out! Now, would you like a boiled egg?”

“Yes please. With no poop in it!”

.o0o.

8. THE CLICKING THING

2016 was the two hundredth anniversary of the writing of Mary Shelley's wonderful story "Frankenstein". There was a world-wide competition to celebrate the occasion - "The Frankenstein Bicentennial Dare". The challenge was to write a thousand words or so on "The relationship between creator and creation."

Maybe it's because I approached the challenge a bit differently. Maybe the judges liked poetry. Or stories written with kids in mind. Anyway, I won.

It was first published on-line on what would have been my Dad's 96th birthday. There's a fair bit of him in the story - I like to think he'd get a kick out of it.

A remarkable inventor was Professor
  Thaddeus Plumpton-Green,
The man who was responsible for a
  most unique machine.

It turned out to be one of the best the
    world had ever seen.

He wasn't very popular with other
    scientific brains.
They thought him odd, old-fashioned,
    and not up with modern gains
And in return he thought them trapped
    in unimaginative chains.

How things should work was what the
    Prof and his colleagues most would
    clash on.
Electronic new technology and
    computers may be fashion
But he didn't care – gears and springs
    and clockwork were his passion.

He worked with cogs and wheels and
    springs and widgets made of tin.
Rack and pinion joints, and spools,
    and wire he'd coil around a pin
And the hammering of metal sheets
    that created quite a din.

The sound of his constructions could
  be as loud as you'd predict
So he lived and worked outside of
  town where the noise rules weren't
  so strict,
And in that lab he called his home, he
  built the Thing that clicked.

Although he lived all by himself he
  seldom felt alone.
So much went on inside his head – a
  heavy traffic zone
But the Thing that clicked was
  company, in a way he'd never
  known.

Of course it could do more than click,
  if given half a chance.
It could nod and bow, and smile and
  wave. It could walk and run and
  prance.
When it was moved a special way the
  Thing would even dance.

That delighted old Prof P, who'd
 dance when on his own
To foxtrot records, classic jazz, on his
 wind-up gramophone.
If he tripped, or didn't keep in time,
 the Thing would never moan.

Its clicking fitted with the jazz, in
 rhythm with the beat.
A dance partner who did not complain
 was, for clumsy Prof, a treat
For the Thing, it didn't feel a thing if
 he trampled on its feet!

Once he told his Thing a joke and it
 gave him back a wink. It
Startled Plumpton-Green. He loved
 his animated trinket
But to call it 'life' was just too much –
 best not overthink it!

He hadn't made a monster, of that he
 was quite certain.
The Thing was all of clockwork with

no feelings to be hurting,
But Plumpton-Green still fretted as he
    peeped out round his curtain.

He went into town as he sometimes
    did to buy food, supplies and tools
When he saw some children as they
    walked to playgrounds or to schools.
"If they like my Thing I'm safe," he
    thought, "For the young are no-one's
    fools!"

Back in his lab he made more Things
    – just a few at first to share.
No monsters these, but playmates,
    each made with skill and care.
"If these kids like them I'll make
    more for children everywhere!"

He took the new Things into town and
    gave them out for free
They clicked as they ran and danced
    and played and filled young hearts
    with glee

And parents seemed quite satisfied
  with his safety guarantee.

As children played with their clicking
  Things two men in suits walked by.
The fun the children clearly had
  caught one shrewd man's cold eye.
He nudged his pal, said: "The next big
  thing! Let's get rich, you and I!"

The men in suits were already rich
  from selling other stuff
But the funny thing with money is for
  some, there's never enough.
When Professor P. said, "Not for
  sale!" they left him in a huff.

They found a boy who swapped
  his Thing for a computer game and
  sweets.
The lazy lad would rather play inside
  than on the streets
And the company of friends was less
  important than his treats.

So the men in suits had got their
    Thing and hardly spent a penny.
They had plenty cash, and grand
    ideas, but morals? Hardly any.
"If a few of these are such big hits,
    what dough we'll make with many!"

"We can make more faster, cheaper,
    better too when we understand the
    trick!"
So their smart guys took the Thing
    apart to see what made it tick.
They even found the little bit that had
    given it its click.

They built a grand new factory with
    machines all big and fine,
Even automated polishers to give a
    brilliant shine
To New Improved Things by the
    thousand, off a huge production line.

Professor Plumpton read a press
    release of what the men in suits

would do.
They'd flood the market with new
    Things, click-free, and cheaper, too.
He sighed and patted Thing the First
    and said, "At least I've still got you."

But the New Improved Things didn't
    sell – no-one wanted them as toys.
"What's wrong with them? What's
    wrong with you?" the men asked
    girls and boys.
The answer came, "They're not the
    same. We <u>liked</u> the clicking noise!"

The men in suits were horrified at
    what the children spoke.
The factory, sales plan, marketing had
    all gone up in smoke.
Their production line of monsters left
    the men in suits quite broke.

The men in suits sold all their Things
    to the sheikh of a far-off land
Who used them as cheap labour to

construct his buildings grand.
But alas, they didn't last for long as
   their gears were clogged with sand.

Tastes change quickly nowadays and
   novelty wears thin.
Even those few Things that clicked
   were soon no longer 'in'.
But the Prof back in his lab still wore
   his quiet contented grin.

For he still had his Thing the First to
   proudly call his own.
They'd stay up late and dance to jazz
   on the trusty gramophone,
As years went by old Plumpton-Green
   never had to be alone.

When the old Professor passed away,
   the Thing it couldn't cry.
It didn't have the means for tears,
   however it may try.
It hadn't been designed to weep or
mourn or even sigh.

It held his body to its breast and
  danced a gentle sway.
The music stopped, the Thing still
  moved in a tender, loving way
Until the gears at last wound down,
  and the last click died away.

.oOo.

9. THE TRIBE THAT LOST A PIECE OF THEIR SOUL AND DISCOVERED A WORLD

Any sufficiently advanced technology is indistinguishable from magic, or so I've been told. That can work two ways.

The 'modern world' is so in awe of technology and the pace that it's developing at that many people dismiss old cultures and old ways. People say 'primitive' like it's a bad thing.

My answer to that is 'don't knock what you don't understand'.

William Bowmore Wise liked to travel, and he liked to take pictures.

He especially liked to take pictures with his very expensive and very clever mobile phone that had a very clever camera built into it. He had a big

camera too, but his phone was easier
to carry around.

William B. Wise lived in a big city in
Australia, but he really liked to travel.

Fortunately he was quite rich, so he
could afford to visit a lot of interesting places.

William liked taking pictures of people who had less than he did because
he thought they were interesting. He
wasn't being smug or unkind. He just
didn't quite understand them.

He'd always been quite rich and
didn't know what it was like to have
to make his own clothes or bake his

own bread. He couldn't imagine what
it must be like to grow his own food
or catch his own fish or build his own
house.

William didn't even really understand
what it was like to have to work hard
to have enough money to buy food or
a place to live.

He took pictures of people working
and building and fishing and farming
because they were things that to him
were different and unusual.

When William took pictures of people, he didn't think of them as people. It was like they were just things.
Things to take pictures of, just like

bridges and buildings and sunflowers
and sunsets.

*

The Williwilli people were a very
small, very ancient tribe who lived in
Central Australia.

There weren't many of them any
more. They didn't have a home.
They hadn't had a home for thousands
of years.

The Williwilli people were nomads.
They wandered from place to place,
and built rough shelters to sleep in
for just as long as they stayed in one
place.

Sometimes they would hunt, sometimes they would fish, and sometimes
they would gather the fruits and plants
that grew in what other people called
the Outback.

The Williwilli people knew a little
about things like cars and cameras and
computers. They'd seen them when
they happened to be at a place where
there were tourists visiting.

They knew about such things, but
they weren't very interested in them.

Those were things that the Williwilli
people had never had, so they never
missed having them. They were quite
content with their lives and the way

that they lived them.

But one thing that none of the Williwilli people liked was to have their
picture taken.

They really *really* believed that if
someone took a picture of you then
they took a piece of your soul. That
was the thing inside you that made
You who you were, and if someone
took a piece of it then you would be
less You.

*

One day William B. Wise was on a
trip to Central Australia. The tour
guide took William and some other

people out into the desert to see "one of the real old tribes".

It was the Williwilli people. They had set up their little camp near a tiny billabong that they'd visited many times over many years. They knew it was the right season to gather some especially nice berries that grew on little bushes beside the water of that billabong.

Before the tourists got off of their bus the tour guide told William and the others in the group, "I must warn you that the people in this tribe do not like to have their pictures taken. They think that takes away a piece of their soul."

William thought that was a very peculiar idea. He didn't want to upset the people he hadn't met yet, so he decided to leave his big camera on the bus.

But as he walked around the camp watching the Williwilli he thought that what they were doing was very interesting.

William thought to himself, "I'll use the camera in my mobile phone. If they don't see me taking pictures they won't be upset."

So he walked around the camp, smiling at people and secretly taking their pictures.

He took pictures of children playing, and old people sitting under trees. He took pictures of mothers nursing their babies, and men weaving grass into baskets to hold the berries they collected.

Nobody noticed what William was doing.

Soon he had taken pictures of nearly everyone in the little Williwilli tribe. He was very pleased, and waved happily to them as he got back on the bus to leave with the tour guide.

The Williwilli people just got on with their day. The visit from the tourists was something that had happened

before. It was just one more thing
that happened to them sometimes, and
they adapted to it.

But the next day, when they woke up
with the sunrise, they knew something
felt wrong. All the tribe, young and
old and in-between, looked at each
other, a little bit worried. It felt like
they weren't quite all there.

*

Inside William's very clever mobile
phone, something very strange was
happening.

All the little pieces of the souls of the
Williwilli tribe were in there.

Because they really *really* believed
that this was what happened when
someone took your picture, whether
you knew about it or not.

And because they were all the same
tribe, and the tribe being very ancient
had been together for a very long
time, those little pieces of soul started
to talk to each other.

The babies talked to their mothers.
The men talked to the women. The
old people and the children talked to
everybody.

On their own, none of the little bits of
soul would have been able to do anything much. But all of them shared a

lifetime of experience at being Willi-willi, however long that lifetime had been. And all together, they could do something special.

They got together inside the camera inside the very clever mobile phone, and the pieces of the tribe became a new kind of living thing. They started to explore.

For thousands of years the Williwilli tribe had wandered around Australia, surviving by adapting to their environment. Wherever they went they explored the place and tried to understand how it worked, so they could make the most of it.

Most importantly, they worked out how best to make themselves safe. That was how the Williwilli tribe had survived for so long.

They studied the plants and animals to find what was best to eat, and when it was easiest to find. They studied the leaves and bark and stones to work out what each could be used for. They carefully studied the weather so they could tell where best to put up their shelters and make their fires out of strong winds.

Now they were together inside the camera inside the very clever mobile phone, and so they started to study the strange electronic world around them.

It took some time, because everything was quite different to anything
they'd ever experienced before. But it
was a very clever phone, and perhaps
it helped them a little bit.

*

The first time William Bowmore
Wise realised something strange was
happening was a couple of weeks later
when he tried to show a friend some
of the pictures he'd taken in Central
Australia.

"This is some men weaving bags out
of leaves," he said, handing the very
clever phone to his friend without
looking at it himself.

His friend looked puzzled and replied, "It's a picture of some sand."

William looked at the picture on the
screen, and sure enough, there was
only sand to be seen.

"I was sure that was the picture of the
men weaving," he said.

Then he scrolled to the next picture.
All he could see was the bottom of a
tree.

"I'm sure there was a group of old
people in that picture! They were
sitting together talking!" he said.

His friend chuckled and said, "I

thought you were a better photogra-
pher than that, William."

William B. Wise scratched his head
and said, "There must be something
wrong with my phone. I'll look at it
later."

But there was nothing wrong with
the very clever phone. It was just that
all the pieces of Williwilli soul that
had gotten together happened to be
exploring just when William tried to
show their pictures, so they weren't
where they used to be.

They were working out how this
strange new environment worked, and
how to make sure that they were safe.

So when William B. Wise decided that some of his Central Australian pictures weren't at all what he wanted and tried to delete them from his very clever mobile phone, he found that he couldn't.

The Williwilli had found a way to build a shelter around the little place inside the camera where they lived. So when the *Delete* function blew over them like a sandstorm or a strong westerly wind, they were quite safe.

William frowned at his very clever phone and shook his head. He decided to turn off the phone and try again later. But of course by the time it was later, he'd forgotten all about deleting any of the pictures.

Of course, turning off the very clever phone didn't affect the Williwilli. It never affected the little clock that always kept time. It didn't affect any of the pictures that were stored in the phone's memory, or the list of friends' phone numbers. It never affected any of the text messages that were stored.

While the phone was switched off, the Williwilli weren't. They explored everything they could find, and studied how to make it all work.

*

Exploring the other pictures on the

camera had been interesting for the Williwilli. The tribe had always been wanderers, visiting new places, and now they were discovering that there was a whole world outside Australia.

The tribe had seen the desert, and the bush. Some had seen mountains and even the coast as they had wandered during the years. But none of them could remember seeing anywhere but Australia. That was where the Williwilli had wandered for thousands of years.

Now they were finding out about India, and South Africa, and Norway. Places where William B. Wise had visited and taken pictures that he'd never gotten around to deleting from his very clever mobile phone.

They found other things too, like William's bank account, and all they needed to know about a very useful person called Travel Agent on William's contact list.

*

Soon after, William B. Wise received a message from his travel agent confirming the trip to Norway that he had booked and paid for.

"That's strange," said William to himself. "I don't remember doing that."

He was just about to call the travel agent to cancel the trip when his very clever phone beeped. It was the special beep that meant a text message had arrived for him.

William looked at the screen. It told him that the message had come from his own very clever phone.

"This is getting stranger and stranger!" said William Bowmore Wise.

He opened the message.

It said LET US GO TO NORWAY.

William looked at the message for a long time. He put the phone down,

walked away, and made a cup of tea
for himself.

Then he sat drinking his tea and looking at the message.

When his cup was empty, he
scratched his head and sent a message
of his own.

It said WHY NORWAY?

Moments later the very clever phone
beeped again.

The new message said WANT TO
SEE SNOW.

William looked at his very clever

phone. He looked worried. Could his phone be alive?

 He typed **WHO ARE YOU?** Before he could send the message the screen cleared and a reply appeared.

 WILLIWILLI it said.

 William asked **THAT'S A TYPE OF WIND ISN'T IT?**

 PEOPLE. TRIBE. YOU TOOK US.

 Once again, William B. Wise put down his phone and walked away. He stood and looked out of the window of his nice expensive house for a very

long time. He was thinking. Thinking about things he'd never thought of
before.

*

All that night, and well into the next
morning before he got much too tired,
William Bowmore Wise sat up typ-
ing and reading messages on his very
clever phone. He was running out of
energy so he had to go to sleep for a
while.

The battery in the phone got low on
power just like William, and it had to
be recharged too. The thing that was
pieces of the souls of the Williwilli
didn't get tired.

When William woke up he didn't rush to his very clever phone. He hadn't slept very well. He'd felt guilty about stealing pieces of the Williwilli's souls.

He hadn't meant to, and he still wasn't quite sure how it was possible. But the Williwilli believed it, and that was what mattered.

The Williwilli didn't seem angry at him. He was a bit surprised and a bit relieved about that. They, or should he call it 'he', or even 'it' – no, 'they' felt more polite – they seemed too interested in exploring to be upset.

William had a shower and ate a very

late breakfast – so late he could have called it lunch. Only after that did he feel that he was ready to look at the phone.

Perhaps he'd dreamed it all.

He typed a message that read ARE YOU THERE, WILLIWILLI?

YES came the answer.

William smiled. Then he typed LET'S GO EXPLORE THE WORLD!

*

William B. Wise took his very clever

phone to Norway. The Williwilli saw
snow – lots of it!

It was dark nearly all the time while
they were there. The sun only peeped
a little way over the horizon for an
hour or so in the middle of the day.

There was a hotel carved out of ice,
and beautiful coloured lights that
danced in the clear dark sky.

William took the very clever phone
to Africa. The Williwilli saw animals
that they could hardly have imagined.

They saw giraffes, and elephants,
and antelopes with great long curved
horns, and even a hippopotamus.

There were some tribes of people there who were as dark or darker than the Williwilli. Some of them didn't want their pictures taken because they also believed that would mean taking a piece of their souls.

This time, William B. Wise respected that wish. Having more than one tribe living in it could be too confusing even for his very clever mobile phone!

William took the very clever phone to New York. The Williwilli saw buildings taller than any mountain that the tribe had ever known.

There were trains that went under

ground and neon lights so bright it
seemed the city could never sleep.

The Williwilli had only ever known
the didgeridoo and rhythm sticks, so
all the different types of music, from
an orchestra to a jazz band to a gui-
tarist playing a rock song on a street
corner, were very exciting.

William took the very clever phone
to China. The Williwilli saw a wall
so huge that you could see it from the
Moon.

There were lots and lots of people
living crowded together in the city.
It seemed like the whole of the tribe
would have been squeezed into one

house if they'd wanted to live there.

William took the very clever phone
to Greece. The Williwilli saw groves
of olive trees that some Greek people
said never died – they just got slowly
older and greyer.

There were buildings like the Acrop-
olis and the Parthenon that were
nearly as old as the tribe. But over the
thousands of years the buildings had
become ruins and fallen apart. The
tribe was still together.

*

After visiting Greece that thought
bothered William B. Wise.

"The tribe are still together, except for the bits of their souls that I took," he said to himself. "I wonder if I can put them back together?"

William made a plan, and arranged everything carefully NOT using his very clever mobile phone. He wanted it to be a surprise.

A few weeks later he got out of a little aeroplane he'd hired to take him way out into Central Australia.

He switched his very clever phone back on, and typed the word SUR-PRISE! Right away he took some pictures of the desert so the Williwilli would know where they were.

WHY ARE WE HERE?

William typed SO I CAN PUT THE TRIBE BACK TOGETHER.

What appeared on the screen was ?????

William tried to explain his idea. IF I SHOW THE PICTURES OF YOU TO YOUR REAL SELVES PER-HAPS THE PIECES OF SOUL WILL GO BACK WHERE THEY CAME FROM.

There was a long pause before the reply came – PERHAPS?

It took a day or two to find the people

of the Williwilli tribe. They were out
in the desert a little way, near some
trees that they knew had good wood
for making new spears with.

 William Bowmore Wise sat down
with some of the people in the tribe.
He explained that he was very sorry,
but he had accidently stolen some of
their souls. He would like to give
them back, if he could.

 Some of the people were quite angry,
but William was so clearly very sorry
they tried to forgive him.

But there was a problem.

It had been a long time since William

had last been in Central Australia.
Time enough to have travelled the
world. Time enough to visit many
places including Norway and Africa, New York and China and even
Greece.

 The babies in William's pictures
weren't babies any more. The little
children playing in the pictures were
now hunting and gathering and making things for themselves.

 Some of the men and women in
William's pictures weren't with each
other any more. Worst of all, some of
the people in the pictures, young and
old and in between, had died. All that
was left of them was what was taken

in the pictures.

"We have learned to live with our loss, even though we didn't know quite what had happened," one old Williwilli woman explained.

"We have become what we are now without those pieces. It's like losing a finger, or an eye. You're not all that you were, but you are still You, and you go on," she said.

 William looked at the people of the Williwilli tribe, and how they had all aged since he'd seen them last. Then he looked at the very clever phone.

 He realised that the bits of soul that

made up the new thing in his phone
hadn't aged, although the thing that
they'd become had certainly learned
and gotten wiser.

 Before he got back onto the little
aeroplane William typed DO YOU
WANT TO TRY TO COME OUT?

 NO. WILLIWILLI ALWAYS MOVE
ON. ALWAYS EXPLORE.

 William nodded. He'd been learning,
too, as he travelled. He turned the
very clever phone around, held it at
arm's length and with its camera he
took a 'selfie'. His own picture was
taken. Now he knew what that meant.

The next morning William Bowmore Wise woke up in the nice hotel in Central Australia that he'd arranged to stay in. He felt not quite himself, like he wasn't all there.

But he knew what he had to do. He downloaded all the pictures on his very clever phone onto the hotel's computer, first making very sure that it was connected to the Internet. The Internet that connected the whole planet – so that they would be living world wide, never running out of new places to wander and explore.

WilliWilly was loose on the world!

.o0o.

10. HAPPILY EVER AFTER

This started with a conversation I heard one evening. A little girl wanted to watch a DVD of a 'classic old fairy story'. Her Mum was in an unhappy mood. I think she'd had an argument with someone earlier that day.

We can't change what other people do or say. We can only control how we react - how we let them affect us.

It's up to you - how do <u>you</u> want to live?

"There's no such thing as living
  happily ever after!"
said a mother to her children.

"You shouldn't read silly stories that
  tell you such untruths!"
"Bad things happen to good people!"
"You'll be disappointed!"
"Promises get broken, and things
  end!"

All of that is true, of course.
But remember this, my friends:

Living happily is not the same as
  being happy all the time.

Sometimes you will be hurt.
Sometimes people will upset you,
  or let you down.
Even your friends and the people you
  care about.

But there is always someone who
  loves you.

They may be right beside you.
Or they may live in your memory and
  your heart.
Or you may not have met them yet.
But they're there.

There is still beauty in the world.
Beautiful places, beautiful things,
  beautiful people.

Look out for them.
Find them, and cherish them.
Remember the things that have been
  good.
Believe that there will always be
  more.

Live happily. Ever after.

.oOo.

For more of Renoir's work visit
www.renoirwords.com

Urban fantasy -
the *Dubious Magic* books:

THE WIZARD OF WARAMANGA
THE CARVINGS OF COBBEMARMOO
THE MAD MACHINES OF MUNDARA
THE WARRIORS OF WIWO'OLE
THE SPIRITS OF SRON DUBH

Anecdotes and yarns:

THESE OLD BASTARDS...*

*Profits go to charity - the Australasian
Order of Old Bastards - fighting cancer and
helping kids in hospital!*

Men's Health:

MID-LIFE CRISIS **MAN**AGEMENT
- A Blokes' Guide To Surviving
Middle Age and Male Menopause